Too Much Trouble

Ruskin Bond has been writing for over sixty years, and now has over 120 titles in print—novels, collections of short stories, poetry, essays, anthologies and books for children. His first novel, *The Room on the Roof*, received the prestigious John Llewellyn Rhys Prize in 1957. He has also received the Padma Shri (1999), the Padma Bhushan (2014) and two awards from Sahitya Akademi—one for his short stories and another for his writings for children. In 2012, the Delhi government gave him its Lifetime Achievement Award.

Born in 1934, Ruskin Bond grew up in Jamnagar, Shimla, New Delhi and Dehradun. Apart from three years in the UK, he has spent all his life in India, and now lives in Mussoorie with his adopted family.

RUSKIN BOND

Too Much Trouble

RUPA

Published by
Rupa Publications India Pvt. Ltd 2006
7/16, Ansari Road, Daryaganj
New Delhi 110002

Sales centres:
Bengaluru Chennai
Hyderabad Jaipur Kathmandu
Kolkata Mumbai Prayagraj

P-ISBN: 978-81-291-0925-5
E-ISBN: 978-81-291-2255-1

Seventeenth impression 2024

20 19 18 17

The moral right of the author has been asserted.

Typeset by Mindways Design, New Delhi

Printed in India

Ghost Trouble

Chapter 1

It was Grandfather who finally decided that we would have to move to another house.

And it was all because of a Pret, a mischievous north-Indian ghost, who had been making life difficult for everyone.

Prets usually live in peepal trees, and that's where our little ghost first had his home—in the branches of a massive old peepal tree which had grown through the compound wall and spread into our garden. Part of the tree was on our side of the wall, part on the other side, shading the main road. It gave the ghost a good view of the whole area.

For many years the Pret had lived there quite happily, without bothering anyone in our house.

It did not bother me, either, and I spent a lot of time in the peepal tree. Sometimes I went there to escape the adults at home, sometimes to watch the road and the people who passed by. The peepal tree was cool on a hot day, and the heart-shaped leaves were always revolving in the breeze. This constant movement of the leaves also helped to disguise the movements of he Pret, so that I never really knew exactly where the was sitting. But he paid no attention to me. The traffic on the road kept him fully occupied.

Sometimes, when a tonga was passing, he would jump down and frighten the pony, and as a result the little pony-cart would go rushing off in the wrong direction.

Sometimes he would get into the engine of a car or a bus, which would have a breakdown soon afterwards.

And he liked to knock the sun-helmets off the heads of sahibs or officials, who would wonder how a strong breeze had sprung up so suddenly, only to die down just as quickly. Although this special kind of ghost could make himself felt, and sometimes heard, he was invisible to the human eye.

I was not invisible to the human eye, and often got the blame for some of the Pret's pranks. If bicycle-riders were struck by mango seeds or apricot stones, they would look up, see a small boy in the branches of the tree, and threaten me with terrible consequences. Drivers who went off after parking their cars in the shade would sometimes come back to find their tyres flat. My protests of innocence did not carry much weight. But when I mentioned the Pret in the tree, they would look uneasy, either because they thought I must be mad, or because they were afraid of ghosts, especially Prets. They would find other things to do and hurry away.

At night no one walked beneath the peepal tree.

It was said that if you yawned beneath the tree, the Pret would jump down your throat and give you a pain. Our gardener, Chandu, who was always taking sick-leave, blamed the Pret for his tummy troubles. Once, when yawning, Chandu had forgotten to put his hand in front of his mouth, and the ghost had got in without any trouble.

Now Chandu spent most of his time lying on a string-bed in the courtyard of his small house. When Grandmother went to visit him, he would start groaning and holding his sides, the pain was so bad; but when she went away, he did not fuss so much. He claimed that the pain did not affect his appetite, and he ate a normal diet, in fact a little more than normal—the extra amount was meant to keep the ghost happy!

Chapter 2

'Well, it isn't our fault,' said Grandfather, who had given permission to the Public Works Department to cut the tree, which had been on our land. They wanted to widen the road, and the tree and a bit of our wall were in the way. So both had to go.

Several people protested, including the Raja of Jinn, who lived across the road and who sometimes asked Grandfather over for a game of tennis.

'That peepal tree has been there for hundreds of years,' he said. 'Who are we to cut it down?'

'*We*,' said the Chief Engineer, 'are the P.W.D.'

And not even a ghost can prevail against the wishes of the Public Works Department.

They brought men with saws and axes, and first they lopped all the branches until the poor tree was quite naked. It must have been at this moment that the Pret moved out. Then they sawed away at the trunk until, finally, the great old peepal came crashing down on the road, bringing down the telephone wires and an electric pole in the process, and knocking a large gap in the Raja's garden wall.

It took them three days to clear the road, and during that time the Chief Engineer swallowed a lot of dust and tree-pollen. For months afterwards he complained of a choking feeling, although no doctor could ever find anything in his throat.

'It's the Pret's doing,' said the Raja knowingly. 'They should never have cut that tree.'

Deprived of his tree, the Pret decided that he would live in our house.

I first became aware of his presence when I was sitting on the verandah steps, reading a book. A tiny chuckling sound came from behind me. I looked around, but no one was to be seen. When I returned to my book, the chuckling started again. I paid no attention. Then a shower of rose petals fell softly on to the pages of my open book. The Pret wanted me to know he was there!

'All right,' I said. 'So you've come to stay with us. Now let me read.'

He went away then; but as a good Pret has to be bad in order to justify his existence, it was not long before he was up to all sorts of mischief.

He began by hiding Grandmother's spectacles.

'I'm sure I put them down on the dining-table,' she grumbled.

A little later they were found balanced on the snout of a wild boar, whose stuffed and mounted head adorned the verandah wall, a memento of Grandfather's hunting trips when he was young. Naturally, I was at first blamed for this prank. But a day or two later, when the spectacles disappeared again, only to be found dangling from the bars of the parrot's cage, it was agreed that I was not to blame; for the parrot had once bitten off a piece of my finger, and I did not go near it any more.

The parrot was hanging upside down, trying to peer through one of the lenses. I don't know if they improved his vision, but what he saw certainly made him angry, because the pupils of his eyes went very small and he dug his beak into the spectacle frames, leaving them with a permanent dent. I caught them just before they fell to the floor.

But even without the help of the spectacles, it seemed that our parrot could see the Pret. He would keep turning this way and that, lunging out at unseen fingers, and protecting his tail from the tweaks of invisible hands. He had always refused to learn to talk, but now he became quite voluble and began to chatter in some unknown tongue, often screaming with rage and rolling his eyes in a frenzy.

'We'll have to give that parrot away,' said Grandmother. 'He gets more bad-tempered by the day.'

Grandfather was the next to be troubled.

He went into the garden one morning to find all his prize sweet-peas broken off and lying on the grass. Chandu thought the sparrows had destroyed the flowers, but we didn't think the birds could have finished off every single bloom just before sunrise.

'It must be the Pret,' said Grandfather, and I agreed.

The Pret did not trouble me much, because he remembered me from his peepal-tree days and knew I resented the tree being cut as much as he did. But he liked to catch my attention, and he did this by chuckling and squeaking near me when I was alone, or whispering in my ear when I was with someone else. Gradually I began to make out the occasional word. He had started learning English!

Chapter 3

Uncle Benji, who came to stay with us for long periods when he had little else to do (which was most of the time), was soon to suffer.

He was a heavy sleeper, and once he'd gone to bed he hated being woken up. So when he came to breakfast looking bleary-eyed and miserable, we asked him if he was feeling all right.

'I couldn't sleep a wink last night,' he complained. 'Whenever I was about to fall asleep, the bedclothes would be pulled off the bed. I had to get up at least a dozen times to pick them off the floor.' He stared suspiciously at me. 'Where were *you* sleeping last night, young man?'

'In Grandfather's room,' I said. 'I've lent you *my* room.'

'It's that ghost from the peepal tree,' said Grandmother with a sigh.

'Ghost!' exclaimed Uncle Benji. 'I didn't know the house was haunted.'

'It is now,' said Grandmother. 'First my spectacles, then the sweet-peas, and now Benji's bedclothes! What will it be up to next, I wonder?'

We did not have to wonder for long.

There followed a series of minor disasters. Vases fell off tables, pictures fell from walls. Parrots' feathers turned up in the teapot, while the parrot himself let out indignant squawks and swearwords in the middle of the night. Windows which had been closed would be found open, and open windows, closed.

Finally, Uncle Benji found a crow's nest in his bed, and on tossing it out of the window was attacked by two crows.

Then Aunt Ruby came to stay, and things quietened down for a time.

Did Aunt Ruby's powerful personality have an effect on the Pret, or was he just sizing her up?

'I think the Pret has taken a fancy to your aunt,' said Grandfather mischievously. 'He's behaving himself for a change.'

This may have been true, because the parrot, who had picked up some of the English words being tried out by the Pret, now called out, '*Kiss, kiss*,' whenever Aunt Ruby was in the room.

'What a charming bird,' said Aunt Ruby.

'You can keep him if you like,' said Grandmother.

One day Aunt Ruby came in to the house covered in rose petals.

'I don't know where they came from,' she exclaimed. 'I was sitting in the garden, drying my hair, when handfuls of petals came showering down on me!'

'It likes you,' said Grandfather.

'What likes me?'

'The ghost.'

'What ghost?'

'The Pret. It came to live in the house when the peepal tree was cut down.'

'What nonsense!' said Aunt Ruby.

'*Kiss, kiss!*' screamed the parrot.

'There aren't any ghosts, Prets or other kinds,' said Aunt Ruby firmly.

'*Kiss, kiss!*' screeched the parrot again. Or was it the parrot? The sound seemed to be coming from the ceiling.

'I wish that parrot would shut up.'

'It isn't the parrot,' I said. 'It's the Pret.'

Aunt Ruby gave me a cuff over the ear and stormed out of the room.

But she had offended the Pret. From being her admirer, he turned into her enemy. Somehow her toothpaste got switched with a tube of Grandfather's shaving-cream. When she appeared in the dining-room, foaming at the mouth, we ran for our lives, Uncle Benji shouting that she'd got rabies.

Chapter 4

Two days later Aunt Ruby complained that she had been struck on the nose by a grapefruit, which had leapt mysteriously from the pantry shelf and hurled itself at her.

'If Ruby and Benji stay here much longer, they'll both have nervous breakdowns,' said Grandfather thoughtfully.

'I thought they broke down long ago,' I said.

'None of your cheek,' snapped Aunt Ruby.

'He's in league with that Pret to try and get us out of here,' said Uncle Benji.

'Don't listen to him—you can stay as long as you like,' said Grandmother, who never turned away any of her numerous nephews, nieces, cousins or distant relatives.

The Pret, however, did not feel so hospitable, and the persecution of Aunt Ruby continued.

'When I looked in the mirror this morning,' she complained bitterly, 'I saw a little monster, with huge ears, bulging eyes, flaring nostrils and a toothless grin!'

'You don't look *that* bad, Aunt Ruby,' I said, trying to be nice.

'It was either you or that imp you call a Pret,' said Aunt Ruby. 'And if it's a ghost, then it's time we all moved to another house.'

Uncle Benji had another idea.

'Let's drive the ghost out,' he said. 'I know a sadhu who rids houses of evil spirits.'

'But the Pret's not evil,' I said. 'Just mischievous.'

Uncle Benji went off to the bazaar and came back a few hours later with a mysterious long-haired man who claimed to be a sadhu—one who has given up all worldly goods, including most of his clothes.

He prowled about the house, and lit incense in all the rooms, despite squawks of protest from the parrot. All the time he chanted various magic spells.

He then collected a fee of thirty rupees, and promised that we would not be bothered again by the Pret.

As he was leaving, he was suddenly blessed with a shower—no, it was really a downpour—of dead flowers, decaying leaves, orange peel and banana skins. All spells forgotten, he ran to the gate and made for the safety of the bazaar.

Aunt Ruby declared that it had become impossible to sleep at night because of the devilish chuckling that came from beneath her pillow. She packed her bags and left.

Uncle Benji stayed on. He was still having trouble with his bedclothes, and he was beginning to talk to himself, which was a bad sign.

'Talking to the Pret, Uncle?' I asked innocently, when I caught him at it one day.

He gave me a threatening look. 'What did you say?' he demanded. 'Would you mind repeating that?'

I thought it safer to please him. 'Oh, didn't you hear me?' I said. *'Teaching the parrot, Uncle?'*

He glared at me, then walked off in a huff. If he did not leave it was because he was hoping Grandmother would lend him enough money to buy a motorcycle; but Grandmother said he ought to try earning a living first.

One day I found him on the drawing-room sofa, laughing like a madman. Even the parrot was so alarmed that he was silent, head lowered and curious. Uncle Benji was red in the face—literally red all over!

'What happened to your face, Uncle?' I asked.

He stopped laughing and gave me a long hard look. I realized that there had been no joy in his laughter.

'Who painted the wash-basin red without telling me?' he asked in a quavering voice.

As Uncle Benji looked really dangerous, I ran from the room.

'We'll have to move, I suppose,' said Grandfather later. 'Even if it's only for a couple of months. I'm worried about Benji. I've told him that I painted the wash-basin myself but forgot to tell him. He doesn't believe me. He thinks it's the Pret or the boy, or both of them! Benji needs a change. So do we. There's my brother's house at the other end of the town. He won't be using it for a few months. We'll move in next week.'

And so, a few days and several disasters later, we began moving house.

Chapter 5

Two bullock-carts laden with furniture and heavy luggage were sent ahead. Uncle Benji went with them. The roof of our old car was piled high with bags and kitchen utensils. Grandfather took the wheel, I sat beside him, and Granny sat in state at the back.

We set off and had gone some way down the main road when Grandfather started having trouble with the steering-wheel. It appeared to have got loose, and the car began veering about on the road, scattering cyclists, pedestrians, and stray dogs, pigs and hens. A cow refused to move, but we missed it somehow, and then suddenly we were off the road and making for a low wall. Grandfather pressed his foot down on the brake, but we only went faster. 'Watch out!' he shouted.

It was the Raja of Jinn's garden wall, made of single bricks, and the car knocked it down quite easily and went on through it, coming to a stop on the Raja's lawn.

'Now look what you've done,' said Grandmother.

'Well, we missed the flowerbeds,' said Grandfather. 'Someone's been tinkering with the car. Our Pret, no doubt.'

The Raja and two attendants came running towards us.

The Raja was a perfect gentleman, and when he saw that the driver was Grandfather, he beamed with pleasure.

'Delighted to see you, old chap!' he exclaimed. 'Jolly decent of you to drop in. How about a game of tennis?'

'Sorry to have come in through the wall,' apologised Grandfather.

'Don't mention it, old chap. The gate was closed, so what else could you do?'

Grandfather was as much of a gentleman as the Raja, so he thought it only fair to join him in a game of tennis. Grandmother and I watched and drank lemonade. After the game, the Raja waved us goodbye and we drove back through the hole in the wall and out on to the road. There was nothing much wrong with the car.

We hadn't gone far when we heard a peculiar sound, as of someone chuckling and talking to himself. It came from the roof of the car.

'Is the parrot out there on the luggage-rack?' asked Grandfather.

'No,' said Grandmother. 'He went ahead with Benji.'

Grandfather stopped the car, got out, and examined the roof.

'Nothing up there,' he said, getting in again and starting the engine. 'I thought I heard the parrot.'

When we had gone a little further, the chuckling started again. A squeaky little voice began talking in English in the tones of the parrot.

'It's the Pret,' whispered Grandmother. 'What is he saying?'

The Pret's squeak grew louder. 'Come on, come on!' he cried gleefully. 'A new house! The same old friends! What fun we're going to have!'

Grandfather stopped the car. He backed into a driveway, turned round, and began driving back to our old house.

'What are you doing?' asked Grandmother.

'Going home,' said Grandfather.

'And what about the Pret?'

'What about him? He's decided to live with us, so we'll have to make the best of it. You can't solve a problem by running away from it.'

'All right,' said Grandmother. 'But what will we do about Benji?'

'It's up to him, isn't it? He'll be all right if he finds something to do.'

Grandfather stopped the car in front of the verandah steps.

'I'm hungry,' I said.

'It will have to be a picnic lunch,' said Grandmother. 'Almost everything was sent off on the bullock-carts.'

As we got out of the car and climbed the verandah steps, we were greeted by showers of rose petals and sweet-scented jasmine.

'How lovely!' exclaimed Grandmother, smiling. 'I think he likes us, after all.'

Snake Trouble

Chapter 1

After retiring from the Indian Railways and settling in Dehra, Grandfather often made his days (and ours) more exciting by keeping unusual pets. He paid a snake-charmer in the bazaar twenty rupees for a young python. Then, to the delight of a curious group of boys and girls, he slung the python over his shoulder and brought it home.

I was with him at the time, and felt very proud walking beside Grandfather. He was popular in Dehra, especially among the poorer people, and everyone greeted him politely without seeming to notice the python. They were, in fact, quite used to seeing him in the company of strange creatures.

The first to see us arrive was Tutu the monkey, who was swinging from a branch of the jack-fruit tree. One look at the python, ancient enemy of his race, and he fled into the house squealing with fright. Then our parrot, Popeye, who had his perch on the veranda, set up the most awful shrieking and whistling. His whistle was like that of a steam-engine. He had learnt to do this in earlier days, when we had lived near railway-stations.

The noise brought Grandmother to the verandah, where she nearly fainted at the sight of the python curled round Grandfather's neck.

Grandmother put up with most of his pets, but she drew the line at reptiles. Even a sweet-tempered lizard made her blood run cold. There was little chance that she would allow a python in the house.

'It will strangle you to death!' she cried.

'Nonsense,' said Grandfather. 'He's only a young fellow.'

'He'll soon get used to us,' I added, by way of support.

'He might, indeed,' said Grandmother, 'but I have no intention of getting used to him. And your Aunt Ruby is coming to stay with us tomorrow.

She'll leave the minute she knows there's a snake in the house.'

'Well, perhaps we should show it to her first thing,' said Grandfather, who found Aunt Ruby rather tiresome.

'Get rid of it right away,' said Grandmother.

'I can't let it loose in the garden. It might find its way into the chicken shed, and then where will we be?'

'Minus a few chickens,' I said reasonably, but this only made Grandmother more determined to get rid of the python.

'Lock that awful thing in the bathroom,' she said. 'Go and find the man you bought it from, and get him to come here and collect it! He can keep the money you gave him.'

Grandfather and I took the snake into the bathroom and placed it in an empty tub. Looking a bit crestfallen, he said, 'Perhaps your grandmother is right. I'm not worried about Aunt Ruby, but we don't want the python to get hold of Tutu or Popeye.'

We hurried off to the bazaar in search of the snake-charmer but hadn't gone far when we found several snake-charmers looking for us. They had heard that Grandfather was buying snakes, and they had brought with them snakes of various sizes and descriptions.

'No, no!' protested Grandfather. 'We don't want more snakes. We want to return the one we bought.'

But the man who had sold it to us had, apparently, returned to his village in the jungle, looking for another python for Grandfather; and the other snake-charmers were not interested in buying, only in selling. In order to shake them off, we had to return home by a roundabout route, climbing a wall and cutting through an orchard. We found Grandmother pacing up and down the verandah. One look at our faces and she knew we had failed to get rid of the snake.

'All right,' said Grandmother. 'Just take it away yourselves and see that it doesn't come back.'

'We'll get rid of it, Grandmother,' I said confidently. 'Don't you worry.'

Grandfather opened the bathroom door and stepped into the room. I was close behind him. We couldn't see the python anywhere.

'He's gone,' announced Grandfather.

'We left the window open,' I said.

'Deliberately, no doubt,' said Grandmother. 'But it couldn't have gone far. You'll have to search the grounds.'

A careful search was made of the house, the roof, the kitchen, the garden and the chicken shed, but there was no sign of the python.

'He must have gone over the garden wall,' Grandfather said cheerfully. 'He'll be well away by now!'

The python did not reappear, and when Aunt Ruby arrived with enough luggage to show that she had come for a long visit, there was only the parrot to greet her with a series of long, ear-splitting whistles.

Chapter 2

For a couple of days Grandfather and I were a little worried that the python might make a sudden reappearance, but when he didn't show up again we felt he had gone for good. Aunt Ruby had to put up with Toto the monkey making faces at her, something I did only when she wasn't looking; and she complained that Popeye shrieked loudest when she was in the room; but she was used to them, and knew she would have to bear with them if she was going to stay with us.

And then, one evening, we were startled by a scream from the garden.

Seconds later Aunt Ruby came flying up the verandah steps, gasping, 'In the guava tree! I was reaching for a guava when I saw it staring at me. The look in its eyes! As though it would eat me alive—'

'Calm down, dear,' urged Grandmother, sprinkling rose-water over my aunt. 'Tell us, what *did* you see?'

'A snake!' sobbed Aunt Ruby. 'A great boa constrictor in the guava tree. Its eyes were terrible, and it looked at me in such a queer way.'

'Trying to tempt you with a guava, no doubt,' said Grandfather, turning away to hide his smile. He gave me a look full of meaning, and I hurried out into the garden. But when I got to the guava tree, the python (if it had been the python) had gone.

'Aunt Ruby must have frightened it off,' I told Grandfather.

'I'm not surprised,' he said. 'But it will be back, Ranji. I think it's taken a fancy to your aunt.'

Sure enough, the python began to make brief but frequent appearances, usually turning up in the most unexpected places.

One morning I found him curled up on a dressing-table, gazing at his own reflection in the mirror. I went for Grandfather, but by the time we returned the python had moved on.

He was seen again in the garden, and one day I spotted him climbing the iron ladder to the roof. I set off after him, and was soon up the ladder, which I had climbed up many times. I arrived on the flat roof just in time to see the snake disappearing down a drain-pipe. The end of his tail was visible for a few moments and then that too disappeared.

'I think he lives in the drainpipe,' I told Grandfather.

'Where does it get its food?' asked Grandmother.

'Probably lives on those field rats that used to be such a nuisance. Remember, they lived in the drainpipes, too.'

'Hmm…' Grandmother looked thoughtful. 'A snake has its uses. Well, as long as it keeps to the roof and prefers rats to chickens…'

But the python did not confine itself to the roof. Piercing shrieks from Aunt Ruby had us all rushing to her room. There was the python on *her* dressing-table, apparently admiring himself in the mirror.

'All the attention he's been getting has probably made him conceited,' said Grandfather, picking up the python to the accompaniment of further shrieks from Aunt Ruby. 'Would you like to hold him for a minute, Ruby? He seems to have taken a fancy to you.'

Aunt Ruby ran from the room and onto the verandah, where she was greeted with whistles of derision from Popeye the parrot. Poor Aunt Ruby! She cut short her stay by a week and returned to Lucknow, where she was a schoolteacher. She said she felt safer in her school than she did in our house.

Chapter 3

Having seen Grandfather handle the python with such ease and confidence, I decided I would do likewise. So the next time I saw the snake climbing the ladder to the roof, I climbed up alongside him. He stopped, and I stopped too. I put out my hand, and he slid over my arm and up to my shoulder. As I did not want him coiling round my neck, I gripped him with both hands and carried him down to the garden. He didn't seem to mind.

The snake felt rather cold and slippery and at first he gave me goose pimples. But I soon got used to him, and he must have liked the way I handled him, because when I set him down he wanted to climb up my leg. As I had other things to do, I dropped him in a large empty basket that had been left out in the garden. He stared out at me with unblinking, expressionless eyes. There was no way of knowing what he was thinking, if indeed he thought at all.

I went off for a bicycle ride, and when I returned, found Grandmother picking guavas and dropping them into the basket. The python must have gone elsewhere.

When the basket was full, Grandmother said, 'Will you take these over to Major Malik? It's his birthday and I want to give him a nice surprise.'

I fixed the basket on the carrier of my cycle and pedalled off to Major Malik's house at the end of the road. The Major met me on the steps of his house.

'And what has your kind granny sent me today, Ranji?' he asked.

'A surprise for your birthday, sir,' I said, and put the basket down in front of him.

The python, who had been buried beneath all the guavas, chose this moment to wake up and stand straight up to a height of several feet. Guavas tumbled all over the place. The Major uttered an oath and dashed indoors.

I pushed the python back into the basket, picked it up, mounted the bicycle, and rode out of the gate in record time. And it was as well that I did so, because Major Malik came charging out of the house armed with a double-barrelled shotgun, which he was waving all over the place.

'Did you deliver the guavas?' asked Grandmother when I got back.

'I delivered them,' I said truthfully.

'And was he pleased?'

'He's going to write and thank you,' I said.

And he did.

'Thank you for the lovely surprise,' he wrote. *'Obviously you could not have known that my doctor had advised me against any undue excitement. My blood-pressure has been rather high. The sight of your grandson does not improve it. All the same, it's the thought that matters and I take it all in good humour...'*

'What a strange letter,' said Grandmother. 'He must be ill, poor man. Are guavas bad for blood-pressure?'

'Not by themselves, they aren't,' said Grandfather, who had an inkling of what had happened. 'But together with other things they can be a bit upsetting.'

Chapter 4

Just when all of us, including Grandmother, were getting used to having the python about the house and grounds, it was decided that we would be going to Lucknow for a few months.

Lucknow was a large city, about three hundred miles from Dehra. Aunt Ruby lived and worked there. We would be staying with her, and so of course we couldn't take any pythons, monkeys or other unusual pets with us.

'What about Popeye?' I asked.

'Popeye isn't a pet,' said Grandmother. 'He's one of us. He comes too.'

And so the Dehra railway platform was thrown into confusion by the shrieks and whistles of our parrot, who could imitate both the guard's whistle and the whistle of a train. People dashed into their compartments, thinking the train was about to leave, only to realise that the guard hadn't blown his whistle after all. When they got down, Popeye would let out another shrill whistle, which sent everyone rushing for the train again. This happened several times until the guard actually blew his whistle. Then nobody bothered to get on, and several passengers were left behind.

'Can't you gag that parrot?' asked Grandfather, as the train moved out of the station and picked up speed.

'I'll do nothing of the sort,' said Grandmother. 'I've bought a ticket for him, and he's entitled to enjoy the journey as much as anyone.'

Whenever we stopped at a station, Popeye objected to fruit sellers and other people poking their heads in at the windows. Before the journey was over, he had nipped two fingers and a nose, and tweaked a ticket-inspector's ear.

It was to be a night journey, and presently Grandmother covered herself with a blanket and stretched out on the berth. 'It's been a tiring day. I think I'll go to sleep,' she said.

'Aren't we going to eat anything?' I asked.

'I'm not hungry—I had something before we left the house. You two help yourselves from the picnic hamper.'

Grandmother dozed off, and even Popeye started nodding, lulled to sleep by the clackety-clack of the wheels and the steady puffing of the steam-engine.

'Well, I'm hungry,' I said. 'What did Granny make for us?'

'Stuffed samosas, omelettes, and tandoori chicken. It's all in the hamper under the berth.'

I tugged at the cane box and dragged it into the middle of the compartment. The straps were loosely tied. No sooner had I undone them than the lid flew open, and I let out a gasp of surprise.

In the hamper was a python, curled up contentedly. There was no sign of our dinner.

'It's a python,' I said. 'And it's finished all our dinner.'

'Nonsense,' said Grandfather, joining me near the hamper. 'Pythons won't eat omelettes and samosas. They like their food alive! Why, this isn't our hamper. The one with our food in it must have been left behind! Wasn't it Major Malik who helped

41

us with our luggage? I think he's got his own back on us by changing the hamper!'

Grandfather snapped the hamper shut and pushed it back beneath the berth.

'Don't let Grandmother see him,' he said. 'She might think we brought him along on purpose.'

'Well, I'm hungry,' I complained.

'Wait till we get to the next station, then we can buy some pakoras. Meanwhile, try some of Popeye's green chillies.'

'No thanks,' I said. 'You have them, Grandad.'

And Grandfather, who could eat chillies plain, popped a couple into his mouth and munched away contentedly.

*

A little after midnight there was a great clamour at the end of the corridor. Popeye made complaining squawks, and Grandfather and I got up to see what was wrong.

Suddenly there were cries of 'Snake, snake!'

I looked under the berth. The hamper was open.

'The python's out,' I said, and Grandfather dashed out of the compartment in his pyjamas. I was close behind.

About a dozen passengers were bunched together outside the washroom door.

'Anything wrong?' asked Grandfather casually.

'We can't get into the toilet,' said someone. 'There's a huge snake inside.'

'Let me take a look,' said Grandfather. 'I know all about snakes.'

The passengers made way, and Grandfather and I entered the washroom together, but there was no sign of the python.

'He must have got out through the ventilator,' said Grandfather. 'By now he'll be in another compartment!' Emerging from the washroom, he told the assembled passengers 'It's gone! Nothing to worry about. Just a harmless young python.'

When we got back to our compartment, Grandmother was sitting up on her berth.

'I *knew* you'd do something foolish behind my back,' she scolded. 'You told me you'd left that creature behind, and all the time it was with us on the train.'

Grandfather tried to explain that we had nothing to do with it, that this python had been smuggled onto the train by Major Malik, but Grandmother was unconvinced.

'Anyway, it's gone,' said Grandfather. 'It must have fallen out of the washroom window. We're over a hundred miles from Dehra, so you'll never see it again.'

Even as he spoke, the train slowed down and lurched to a grinding halt.

'No station here,' said Grandfather, putting his head out of the window.

Someone came rushing along the embankment, waving his arms and shouting.

'I do believe it's the stoker,' said Grandfather. 'I'd better go and see what's wrong.'

'I'm coming too,' I said, and together we hurried along the length of the stationary train until we reached the engine.

'What's up?' called Grandfather. 'Anything I can do to help? I know all about engines.'

But the engine-driver was speechless. And who could blame him? The python had curled itself about his legs, and the driver was too petrified to move.

'Just leave it to us,' said Grandfather, and, dragging the python off the driver, he dumped the snake in my arms. The engine-driver sank down on the floor, pale and trembling.

'I think I'd better drive the engine,' said Grandfather. 'We don't want to be late getting into Lucknow. Your aunt will be expecting us!' And before the astonished driver could protest, Grandfather had released the brakes and set the engine in motion.

'We've left the stoker behind,' I said.

'Never mind. You can shovel the coal.'

Only too glad to help Grandfather drive an engine, I dropped the python in the driver's lap, and started shovelling coal. The engine picked up speed and we were soon rushing through the darkness, sparks flying skywards and the steam-whistle shrieking almost without pause.

'You're going too fast!' cried the driver.

'Making up for lost time,' said Grandfather. 'Why did the stoker run away?'

'He went for the guard. You've left them both behind!'

Chapter 5

Early next morning the train steamed safely into Lucknow. Explanations were in order, but as the Lucknow station-master was an old friend of Grandfather's, all was well. We had arrived twenty minutes early, and while Grandfather went off to have a cup of tea with the engine-driver and the station-master, I returned the python to the hamper and helped Grandmother with the luggage. Popeye stayed perched on Grandmother's shoulder, eyeing the busy platform with deep distrust. He was the first to see Aunt Ruby striding down the platform, and let out a warning whistle.

Aunt Ruby, a lover of good food, immediately spotted the picnic hamper, picked it up and said,

'It's quite heavy. You must have kept something for me! I'll carry it out to the taxi.'

'We hardly ate anything,' I said.

'It seems ages since I tasted something cooked by your granny.' And after that there was no getting the hamper away from Aunt Ruby.

Glancing at it, I thought I saw the lid bulging, but I had tied it down quite firmly this time and there was little likelihood of its suddenly bursting open.

Grandfather joined us outside the station and we were soon settled inside the taxi. Aunt Ruby gave instructions to the driver and we shot off in a cloud of dust.

'I'm dying to see what's in the hamper,' said Aunt Ruby. 'Can't I take just a little peek?'

'Not now,' said Grandfather. 'First let's enjoy the breakfast you've got waiting for us.'

Popeye, perched proudly on Grandmother's shoulder, kept one suspicious eye on the quivering hamper.

When we got to Aunt Ruby's house, we found breakfast laid out on the dining-table.

'It isn't much,' said Aunt Ruby. 'But we'll supplement it with what you've brought in the hamper.'

47

Placing the hamper on the table, she lifted the lid and peered inside. And promptly fainted.

Grandfather picked up the python, took it into the garden, and draped it over a branch of a pomegranate tree.

When Aunt Ruby recovered, she insisted that she had seen a huge snake in the picnic hamper. We showed her the empty basket.

'You're seeing things,' said Grandfather. 'You've been working too hard.'

'Teaching is a very tiring job,' I said solemnly.

Grandmother said nothing. But Popeye broke into loud squawks and whistles, and soon everyone, including a slightly hysterical Aunt Ruby, was doubled up with laughter.

But the snake must have tired of the joke because we never saw it again!

Monkey Trouble

Chapter 1

Grandfather bought Tutu from a street entertainer for the sum of ten rupees. The man had three monkeys. Tutu was the smallest, but the most mischievous. She was tied up most of the time. The little monkey looked so miserable with a collar and chain that Grandfather decided it would be much happier in our home. Grandfather had a weakness for keeping unusual pets. It was a habit that I, at the age of eight or nine, used to encourage.

Grandmother at first objected to having a monkey in the house. 'You have enough pets as it is,' she said, referring to Grandfather's goat, several white mice, and a small tortoise.

'But I don't have any,' I said.

'You're wicked enough for two monkeys. One boy in the house is all I can take.'

'Ah, but Tutu isn't a boy,' said Grandfather triumphantly. 'This is a little girl monkey!'

Grandmother gave in. She had always wanted a little girl in the house. She believed girls were less troublesome than boys. Tutu was to prove her wrong.

She was a pretty little monkey. Her bright eyes sparkled with mischief beneath deep-set eyebrows. And her teeth, which were a pearly white, were often revealed in a grin that frightened the wits out of Aunt Ruby, whose nerves had already suffered from the presence of Grandfather's pet python. But this was my grandparents' house, and aunts and uncles had to put up with our pets.

Tutu's hands had a dried-up look, as though they had been pickled in the sun for many years. One of the first things I taught her was to shake hands, and this she insisted on doing with all who visited the house. Peppery Major Malik would have to stoop and shake hands with Tutu before he could enter the drawing room, otherwise Tutu would climb onto his shoulder and stay there, roughing up his hair and playing with his moustache.

Uncle Benji couldn't stand any of our pets and took a particular dislike to Tutu, who was always making faces at him. But as Uncle Benji was never in a job for long, and depended on Grandfather's good-natured generosity, he had to shake hands with Tutu, like everyone else.

Tutu's fingers were quick and wicked. And her tail, while adding to her good looks (Grandfather believed a tail would add to anyone's good looks!), also served as a third hand. She could use it to hang from a branch, and it was capable of scooping up any delicacy that might be out of reach of her hands.

On one of Aunt Ruby's visits, loud shrieks from her bedroom brought us running to see what was wrong. It was only Tutu trying on Aunt Ruby's petticoats! They were much too large, of course, and when Aunt Ruby entered the room, all she saw was a faceless white blob jumping up and down on the bed.

We disentangled Tutu and soothed Aunt Ruby. I gave Tutu a bunch of sweet-peas to make her happy. Granny didn't like anyone plucking her sweet-peas, so I took some from Major Malik's garden while he was having his afternoon siesta.

Then Uncle Benji complained that his hairbrush was missing. We found Tutu sunning herself on the back verandah, using the hairbrush to scratch her armpits.

I took it from her and handed it back to Uncle Benji with an apology; but he flung the brush away with an oath.

'Such a fuss about nothing,' I said. 'Tutu doesn't have fleas!'

'No, and she bathes more often than Benji,' said Grandfather, who had borrowed Aunt Ruby's shampoo to give Tutu a bath.

All the same, Grandmother objected to Tutu being given the run of the house. Tutu had to spend her nights in the out-house, in the company of the goat. They got on quite well, and it was not long before Tutu was seen sitting comfortably on the back of the goat, while the goat roamed the back garden in search of its favourite grass.

The day Grandfather had to visit Meerut to collect his railway pension, he decided to take Tutu and me along to keep us both out of mischief, he said. To prevent Tutu from wandering about on the train, causing inconvenience to passengers, she was provided with a large black travelling bag. This, with some straw at the bottom, became her compartment. Grandfather and I paid for our seats, and we took Tutu along as hand baggage.

There was enough space for Tutu to look out of the bag occasionally, and to be fed with bananas and biscuits, but she could not get her hands through the opening and the canvas was too strong for her to bite her way through.

Tutu's efforts to get out only had the effect of making the bag roll about on the floor or occasionally jump into the air—an exhibition that attracted a curious crowd of onlookers at the Dehra and Meerut railway stations.

Anyway, Tutu remained in the bag as far as Meerut, but while Grandfather was producing our tickets at the turnstile, she suddenly poked her head out of the bag and gave the ticket collector a wide grin.

The poor man was taken aback. But, with great presence of mind and much to Grandfather's annoyance, he said, 'Sir, you have a dog with you. You'll have to buy a ticket for it.'

'It's not a dog!' said Grandfather indignantly. 'This is a baby monkey of the species *macacus-mischievous*, closely related to the human species *homus-horriblis!* And there is no charge for babies!'

'It's as big as a cat,' said the ticket collector. 'Cats and dogs have to be paid for.'

'But, I tell you, it's only a baby!' protested Grandfather.

'Have you a birth certificate to prove that?' demanded the ticket collector.

'Next, you'll be asking to see her mother,' snapped Grandfather.

In vain did he take Tutu out of the bag. In vain did he try to prove that a young monkey did not qualify as a dog or a cat or even as a quadruped. Tutu was classified as a dog by the ticket collector, and five rupees were handed over as her fare.

Then Grandfather, just to get his own back, took from his pocket the small tortoise that he sometimes carried about, and said: 'And what must I pay for this, since you charge for all creatures great and small?'

The ticket collector looked closely at the tortoise, prodded it with his forefinger, gave Grandfather a triumphant look, and said, 'No charge, sir. It is not a dog!'

Winters in north India can be very cold. A great treat for Tutu on winter evenings was the large bowl of hot water given to her by Grandfather for a bath. Tutu would cunningly test the temperature with her hand, then gradually step into the bath, first one foot, then the other (as she had seen me doing) until she was in the water upto her neck.

Once comfortable, she would take the soap in her hands or feet and rub herself all over. When the water became cold, she would get out and run as quickly as she could to the kitchen fire in order to dry herself. If anyone laughed at her during this performance, Tutu's feelings would be hurt and she would refuse to go on with the bath.

One day Tutu almost succeeded in boiling herself alive. Grandmother had left a large kettle on the fire for tea. And Tutu, all by herself and with nothing better to do, decided to remove the lid. Finding the water just warm enough for a bath, she got in, with her head sticking out from the open kettle.

This was fine for a while, until the water began to get heated. Tutu raised herself a little. But finding it cold outside, she sat down again. She continued hopping up and down for some time, until Grandmother returned and hauled her, half-boiled, out of the kettle.

'What's for tea today?' asked Uncle Benji gleefully. 'Boiled eggs and a half-boiled monkey?'

But Tutu was none the worse for the adventure and continued to bathe more regularly than Uncle Benji.

Aunt Ruby was a frequent taker of baths. This met with Tutu's approval—so much so that, one day, when Aunt Ruby had finished shampooing her hair, she looked up through a lather of bubbles and soap-suds to see Tutu sitting opposite her in the bath, following her example.

One day Aunt Ruby took us all by surprise. She announced that she had become engaged. We had always thought Aunt Ruby would never marry—she had often said so herself—but it appeared that the right man had now come along in the person of Rocky Fernandes, a schoolteacher from Goa.

Rocky was a tall, firm-jawed, good-natured man, a couple of years younger than Aunt Ruby. He had a fine baritone voice and sang in the manner of the great Nelson Eddy. As Grandmother liked baritone singers, Rocky was soon in her good books.

'But what on earth does he see in her?' Uncle Benji wanted to know.

'More than any girl has seen in you!' snapped Grandmother. 'Ruby's a fine girl. And they're both teachers. Maybe they can start a school of their own.'

Rocky visited the house quite often and brought me chocolates and cashew nuts, of which he seemed to have an unlimited supply. He also taught me several marching songs. Naturally, I approved of Rocky. Aunt Ruby won my grudging admiration for having made such a wise choice.

One day I overheard them talking of going to the bazaar to buy an engagement ring. I decided I would go along, too. But as Aunt Ruby had made it clear that she did not want me around, I decided that I had better follow at a discreet distance. Tutu, becoming aware that a mission of some importance was under way, decided to follow me. But as I had not invited her along, she too decided to keep out of sight.

Once in the crowded bazaar, I was able to get quite close to Aunt Ruby and Rocky without being spotted. I waited until they had settled down in a large jewellery shop before sauntering past and spotting them, as though by accident. Aunt Ruby wasn't too pleased at seeing me, but Rocky waved and called out, 'Come and join us! Help your aunt choose a beautiful ring!'

The whole thing seemed to be a waste of good money, but I did not say so—Aunt Ruby was giving me one of her more unloving looks.

'Look, these are pretty!' I said, pointing to some cheap, bright agates set in white metal. But Aunt Ruby wasn't looking. She was immersed in a case of diamonds.

'Why not a ruby for Aunt Ruby?' I suggested, trying to please her.

'That's her lucky stone,' said Rocky. 'Diamonds are the thing for engagements.' And he started singing a song about a diamond being a girl's best friend.

While the jeweller and Aunt Ruby were sifting through the diamond rings, and Rocky was trying out another tune, Tutu had slipped into the shop without being noticed by anyone but me. A little squeal of delight was the first sign she gave of her presence. Everyone looked up to see her trying on a pretty necklace.

'And what are those stones?' I asked.

'They look like pearls,' said Rocky.

'They *are* pearls,' said the shopkeeper, making a grab for them.

'It's that dreadful monkey!' cried Aunt Ruby. 'I knew that boy would bring him here!'

The necklace was already adorning Tutu's neck. I thought she looked rather nice in them, but she gave us no time to admire the effect. Springing out of our reach, Tutu dodged around Rocky, slipped between my legs, and made for the crowded road. I ran after her, shouting to her to stop, but she wasn't listening.

There were no branches to assist Tutu in her progress, but she used the heads and shoulders of people as springboards and so made rapid headway through the bazaar.

The jeweller left his shop and ran after us. So did Rocky. So did several bystanders, who had seen the incident. And others, who had no idea what it was all about, joined in the chase. As Grandfather used to say, 'In a crowd, everyone plays follow-the-leader, even when they don't know who's leading.' Not everyone knew that the leader was Tutu. Only the front runners could see her.

She tried to make her escape speedier by leaping onto the back of a passing scooterist. The scooter swerved into a fruit stall and came to a standstill under a heap of bananas, while the scooterist found himself in the arms of an indignant fruitseller. Tutu peeled a banana and ate part of it, before deciding to move on.

From an awning she made an emergency landing on a washerman's donkey. The donkey promptly panicked and rushed down the road, while bundles of washing fell by the wayside. The washerman joined in the chase. Children on their way to school decided that here was something better to do than attend classes. With shouts of glee, they soon overtook their panting elders.

Tutu finally left the bazaar and took a road leading in the direction of our house. But knowing that she would be caught and locked up once she got home, she decided to end the chase by ridding herself of the necklace. Deftly removing it from her neck, she flung it in the small canal that ran down the road.

The jeweller, with a cry of anguish, plunged into the canal. So did Rocky. So did I. So did several other people, both adults and children. It was to be a treasure hunt!

Some twenty minutes later, Rocky shouted, 'I've found it!' Covered in mud, water-lilies, ferns and tadpoles, we emerged from the canal, and Rocky presented the necklace to the relieved shopkeeper.

Everyone trudged back to the bazaar to find Aunt Ruby waiting in the shop, still trying to make up her mind about a suitable engagement ring.

Finally the ring was bought, the engagement was announced, and a date was set for the wedding.

'I don't want that monkey anywhere near us on our wedding day,' declared Aunt Ruby.

'We'll lock her up in the out-house,' promised Grandfather. 'And we'll let her out only after you've left for your honeymoon.'

A few days before the wedding I found Tutu in the kitchen, helping Grandmother prepare the wedding cake. Tutu often helped with the cooking and, when Grandmother wasn't looking, added herbs, spices, and other interesting items to the pots—so that occasionally we found a chilli in the custard or an onion in the jelly or a strawberry floating in the chicken soup.

Sometimes these additions improved a dish, sometimes they did not. Uncle Ken lost a tooth when he bit firmly into a sandwich which contained walnut shells.

I'm not sure exactly what went into that wedding cake when Grandmother wasn't looking—she insisted that Tutu was always very well-behaved in the kitchen—but I did spot Tutu stirring in some red chilli sauce, bitter gourd seeds, and a generous helping of egg-shells!

It's true that some of the guests were not seen for several days after the wedding, but no one said anything against the cake. Most people thought it had an interesting flavour.

The great day dawned, and the wedding guests made their way to the little church that stood on the outskirts of Dehra—a town with a church, two mosques, and several temples.

I had offered to dress Tutu up as a bridesmaid and bring her along, but no one except Grandfather thought it was a good idea. So I was an obedient boy and locked Tutu in the out-house. I did, however, leave the skylight open a little. Grandmother had always said that fresh air was good for growing children, and I thought Tutu should have her share of it.

The wedding ceremony went without a hitch. Aunt Ruby looked a picture, and Rocky looked like a film star.

Grandfather played the organ, and did so with such gusto that the small choir could hardly be heard. Grandmother cried a little, I sat quietly in a corner, with the little tortoise on my lap.

When the service was over, we trooped out into the sunshine and made our way back to the house for the reception.

The feast had been laid out on tables in the garden. As the gardener had been left in charge, everything was in order. Tutu was on her best behaviour. She had, it appeared, used the skylight to avail of more fresh air outside, and now sat beside the three-tier wedding cake, guarding it against crows, squirrels and the goat. She greeted the guests with squeals of delight.

It was too much for Aunt Ruby. She flew at Tutu in a rage. And Tutu, sensing that she was not welcome, leapt away, taking with her the top tier of the wedding cake.

Led by Major Malik, we followed her into the orchard, only to find that she had climbed to the top of the jackfruit tree. From there she proceeded to pelt us with bits of wedding cake. She had also managed to get hold of a bag of confetti, and when she ran out of cake she showered us with confetti.

'That's more like it!' said the good-humoured Rocky. 'Now let's return to the party, folks!'

Uncle Benji remained with Major Malik, determined to chase Tutu away. He kept throwing stones into the tree, until he received a large piece of cake bang on his nose. Muttering threats, he returned to the party, leaving the Major to do battle.

When the festivities were finally over, Uncle Benji took the old car out of the garage and drove up the veranda steps. He was going to drive Aunt Ruby and Rocky to the nearby hill resort of Mussoorie, where they would have their honeymoon.

Watched by family and friends, Aunt Ruby climbed into the back seat. She waved regally to everyone. She leant out of the window and offered me her cheek and I had to kiss her farewell. Everyone wished them luck.

As Rocky burst into song, Uncle Benji opened the throttle and stepped on the accelerator. The car shot forward in a cloud of dust.

Rocky and Aunt Ruby continued to wave to us. And so did Tutu, from her perch on the rear bumper! She was clutching a bag in her hands and showering confetti on all who stood in the driveway.

'They don't know Tutu's with them!' I exclaimed.

'She'll go all the way to Mussoorie! Will Aunt Ruby let her stay with them?'

'Tutu might ruin the honeymoon,' said Grandfather. 'But don't worry—our Benji will bring her back!'